RULES, RULES, RULES!

MARK H. McCRAW

Dedication

This book is dedicated to
Meaghan McCraw -Teal.

ISBN: **979-8-9858936-7-0**

Permission to use material from other works: www.istockphoto.com

Credits for illustrations or photos: www.istockphoto.com

Credits for cover design : www.fiverr.com (amy_creative)

Printed in the United States of America.

For more information or requests, please email the author at worldprofessor1@gmail.com .

This Book Belongs To:

____

Today is the first day of school.

For everything, there is a rule!
Rules! Rules! Rules!

On the Bus:

Nobody is standing in the seats.

The bus driver always repeats.

For class, recess, lunchroom, and halls. How can I remember them all?

My teacher has a lengthy list
but I know there is a twist.

I can only remember a few
because I am so new.

No talking aloud

because the classroom is a zone

when the teacher is on the phone.

In class, we shouldn't play around. We must listen to the teacher without a sound.

No temper tantrums or putting up a fuss.

No harsh words or a cuss.

No pushing, shoving, or teasing.

The teachers agree this is not pleasing.

My teacher has a rule for us all.

However, I am daydreaming about being outside wanting to play with a ball.

If I can remember the rules that others hold so dear,

we will have a good year.

My principal:

There is no chewing, spinning, running, or hitting.

16

As well as no bullying or spitting.

In the lunchroom:

There is absolutely no yelling, throwing, or wasting while eating.

There is no picking your own seating.

There is no sliding upside down. No fighting or being an obnoxious, crazy clown.

In the halls:

We are not running and keeping

our hands to ourselves

while standing tall.

We are all tiptoeing down the hall.

There are so many rules. It is amazing that
I can remember them all.

My bus driver, teacher, cafeteria worker,
principal, and recess monitor expect us

to remember this lengthy list, but when I get

home, it will all be a mist.

I recognize rules make me safe and keep me straight. However, I still get irate.

Until tomorrow... I start right over but I wish everyone would go much slower on the rules

so I can remember them

again.